The
Road
Trip

(Mother and Son's Secret)

Karena Donger

Table of Contents

Content Warning

This book is solely for people who are over the age of legal adulthood due to its sexual content. There are themes with a lot of bad words. All characters are well over the age of eighteen.

"My son's fingers were embedded in my pussy as I spoke to my spouse. "When are we going to come to an end?"

- Ellen

Free Bonus

Grab My "At The Beach (Erotic Romance Story)" Ebook For FREE!

Today you can grab your copy of my Free Erotic Romance story e-book titled – **At The Beach**. Best of all, it won't cost you a thing.

Download and Subscribe for Free book, giveaways, and new releases by **Karena Donger.**

Click the image above to **Download the Book**, and also Subscribe for Free books, giveaways, and new releases by me.

Or Follow the link below;

https://mayobook.com/karenadonger

As my subscriber, you will enjoy more free books exclusive to subscribers only, plus **Free Giveaways**. Wait no further, join my growing number of book lovers, and let's connect.

The Road Trip

In August, we spent the morning getting the car ready for a road trip. Joel, one of our children, was getting ready to head off to college. When I got out of bed, it was already a balmy ninety degrees outside. **Joel** and I worked up a sweat as we piled everything into the car. I couldn't fit any more in my trunk or the backseat. Finally, Joel returned to the house to retrieve all of his personal belongings.

I could hear him coming out of the house as he walked down the driveway. Turning back, I saw him lugging a 42-inch flat-screen TV with him.

"Where will you put the television?" My ears perked up when I heard his dad ask.

In the end, I'm not sure why, but I don't want to give it up. Is there anything we can do to reorganize the backseat?

I took a peek behind the wheel. *"It's not likely, son,"* said the father. **Joel** took a peek inside the vehicle. A middle seat in the front is an option, he said.

We agreed on a time and on a place. Is your mother going to sit there, too?

I could tell he was racking his brains for an answer by the look on his face. He said, *"I've got an idea"* and then proceeded to explain it further.

He let himself out of the car through the passenger door. The television was placed at the center of the car seat by him.

Once inside, he sat down. *"There's plenty of room."* Mom, please take a seat here beside me.

To my son's dismay, I sat next to him. In order to get in, I had to sit down, but the door wouldn't shut properly. I'm no longer a fat woman. I'm a slender five-foot-ten-inch woman who weighs no more than a hundred pounds.

My son was taking up the entire space at the back seat. The young man was already well over six feet tall and weighs about 180 pounds.

Rather than me, it's you who's taking up all the space. This isn't going to succeed. *"When we come to visit you, we'll bring the television with us."*

When I got out of the car and stood by the door, he said, *"No way."*

"Joel, make a decision. It's getting hot out here." I said.

Joel smiled as he nodded and smiled back at me. You're welcome to sit on my lap, mum.

His father told him, *"Joel, it's a five-hour drive to your college."*

It's true, but my mother does not have a huge body frame, I can lap her conveniently sir.

Mom, what do you think? *"Would it be okay if you sat on my lap mum?"* **Joel** asked.

"Let me take a seat on your lap, then." I agreed.

Even if I'd like to stop at a rest stop if the situation gets too uncomfortable. I said this while staring at my spouse. *He nodded his head in agreement.*

It's time to take a shower and get ready for the road trip, right? My asked asked.

There wasn't a lot of time spent in the shower. The five-hour-long ride on my son's lap necessitated that I wear something comfy. My jean pants would be too uncomfortable.

In addition, the weather was unbearably hot. I looked in the closet. While sorting through my wardrobe, I came across a summer dress. There were no sleeves on the short side. In the front, it was buttoned up. I undid the buttons and slipped it on.

As soon as I finished buttoning it, I realized how much of my bra it revealed. I removed it once again. I removed my bra and re-adjusted my dress.

I checked my reflection in the bathroom mirror. I didn't really need a bra at all. My tits were still perky despite being at the age of *thirty-nine*.

It was a short dress. My thighs were barely touched

by it, as the dress was barely covering half of my thigh. *Pear-shaped white panties* were all I needed to complete the look.

For one last time, I examined my reflection. I had a thought. "*As the mother of a twenty years son, I appeared to be in good shape. I'm confident that my husband still appreciates the way I look.*" Five times a week, he fucks me real good!

The car's horn sounded. "puuuuuurrh"

As soon as I got downstairs, I shut and locked the front door of the house, and headed out the door to the car.

My son was already sitting in the car's back seat. I sat down on his lap and swung my legs into the car.

I looked down and *my thighs were barely covered by my clothing because it's short.* It climbed to a respectable altitude of my thigh. Shorts and a t-shirt were all my son had on. I slammed the door of the car.

Wearing this dress made me happy and comfortable

as a beautiful sexy woman.

My son's bare legs touched the back of my legs.

"How are you doing, hope you can bear my weight?" My son was the one I turned to for an answer.

"Okay, mum, you don't weigh much. There is no problem at all."

To my husband's left as we looked over the TV. *Is there enough room for you to drive honey?* I asked him, and he said **yes**.

I could only see his head. *"Can you even see me?"* I laughed as I asked.

"Only your head, dear." "Are you comfortable? he asked."

As I sat on my son's lap, I squirmed around. It's not a problem for me at all.

My husband turned on the radio to play music. A few minutes into the music, something abrasive had begun to gnaw at me. It didn't go away even after I shifted my body position, and adjusted my ass.

In addition, I noticed that my son had been unusually silent. In the beginning, *"I couldn't figure it out."* I had a thought.

It dawned on me that my feelings were not what they seemed to be at the time. <u>My son was having a serious erection by sitting on his lap</u>, I really didn't think about giving him an erection by sitting on his lap.

Even now, I could sense its expansion.

"My gosh,"

I muttered under my breath.

The question is, *"How big will it get?"* I couldn't help but wonder what was going through his mind.

Does he think I can't feel it in my ass?

My gaze was drawn to my legs. There was a slight rise in the skirt of my dress. *I was almost able to see my panties.*

On either side of me, I could see my son's hands resting on the seats.

I was curious if he had noticed how high my dress had ridden up on the back of the chair. I've come to appreciate having my dress so high. Knowing I could give my son a hard-on to make me feel good.

It was just over an hour into our journey. Even with the remaining time, only four hours remained.

In order to avoid my husband noticing how high the skirt of my dress was, I made sure he couldn't see the length of my skirt. He couldn't see anything because of the television in between.

My son's body began to *wiggle*, and I knew it was him.

My ass ended up completely covered on his dick as he did it. I was hoping he would at least give it a go.

Inquiring about how he was doing back there "*son, how are you doing there*".

In response to the question,

"I am Okay mom", "How are you feeling, Mom?"

I told him, "I like what I'm feeling."

I answered him - "Are your arms getting tired where you have them?"

"Yea, it's a little uncomfortable,"

Weird, to say the least.

To see whether it felt better, I took both of his hands and placed them on my bare thighs, saying;

"Is that better"

Yeah, it's much better and more comfortable; He said.

"That's much better, Yes."

I lowered my gaze and took a closer look. When he placed his hands on my thighs, I made sure they were palms down instead of up.

I could feel his thumbs pressing into the crooks of my thighs, very close to my panties. It had a pleasing appearance to me. I wished he'd put his hands on my pussy and stroked it.

In my mind, he couldn't do it. I wanted him to feel me more and more as I felt his hands on me. In my hands, he was mine. All of that appeared to be innocent. I began scrubbing his palms. Like every other mother, I wanted to do something special. My hubby was driving and more focused on the road as the situation was getting sweeter at the back seat of the car.

Having my son's hands on my body was a pleasant thought, especially with my husband around. His hands were moving up my thighs as I stroked them. He didn't resist. His fingers were still on my thighs as he placed his hands on my skirt.

I moved up slightly so that I could raise my skirt a bit. With my skirt, he moved his hands. *My pants were clearly visible when I lowered my gaze. His fingers were just a few centimeters away from my pussy.*

In order to get him to put his right hand on my panties, I raised it, and placed his hand on my panty-covered pussy.

This is where his hand was left. My legs were a little open.

When I did, he reached out and grabbed hold of my panties. I grabbed his hand and pressed it against my panties. My son's hand was now resting on my pussy, which was dripping wet.

I could tell that I was getting wet already. I was starving for more.

When I took my hand off of him, he continued to hold on. He wasn't even fumbling with it. Just letting his hands rest on my pantie-covered pussy, that's all. I waited for him to start moving his fingers.

Nothing happened. Maybe he was afraid to. I knew how to fix that.

When I grabbed his hand, I shifted it up to the top of my underwear. It was only then that I held his hand against mine and allowed him to softly slide his fingers between my undergarments and my exposed fleshy pussy.

When his fingertips finally touched the top of my swollen, pussy lips, **I froze.**

I continued to press my fingers into his palm. The only way he could feel my genitals was if I could slide his hand all the way between my legs and beneath my underpants.

Both of our hands were squeezing out of my pants since they were too small. Then, finally, I felt him try to move his hand farther down so that he could locate my pussy entry point.

My son's hand remained on my genitals as I removed my hand from under my underpants.

With both hands, I lifted my hips and dragged my pants down to my knees. As soon as I did this, I felt Joel move his hand so he could insert his fingers into my pussy.

Because of my underwear, I couldn't get my legs out wide enough for him to truly get a feel for me.

Joel grabbed hold of my pants with his other hand before I could even begin to remove them from around my ankles.

I swung my legs up to make it easier for him to remove them completely. I splayed my legs out as wide as I could.

He didn't need anything else. He slipped two fingers inside me at once since I was so drenched. *A low moan escaped my lips.*

My spouse inquired, *"Are you alright?"* He was glancing my way.

It's OK; *"I thought sitting on my son's lap would be an issue, but it truly is not."* I answered with a smile.

"It won't be too horrible," He says.

My son's fingers were embedded in my pussy as I spoke to my spouse.

"When are we going to come to an end of this road trip?"

He said, *"I don't want to stop until I'm a bit further*

down the road."

I turned to my son in a soft voice,

"I'd want to see a little more from you, Joel."

Mom, you're right. As far as I'm concerned, *"I'm capable of much more."*

"That's good," I said.

"The more time we spend together, the more I enjoy it."

"Is it all right with you, honey?" My husband chimed in.

The thought of never stopping appeals to me. He responded.

To see my son's reaction, I spun around. *"As long as you keep going, I don't want to stop."*

"Joel?" my husband asked my son, *"How are you doing with your mom on your lap?"*

"No problem dad, mom keeps moving around so one position doesn't get uncomfortable. She raises up every

As my son was talking to his dad, he was sinking his fingers even deeper in my pussy.

Joel's fingers were moving in and out of my wet pussy.

To prevent a groan, I bit my tongue. I put my hand on his shoulder. I pushed his hand hard into my pussy. That was something I wanted him to know. His fingers went deep into my pussy.

To the beat of his fingers, *I began swaying my hips.* My hubby was staring at me. It was fortunate that the television was in the way of his view. I don't know what he would do if he could see his son with his fingers buried in his mother's pussy.

My entire body was responding to his touch. He suddenly yanked his fingers away from my pussy. I was let down.

That was short-lived. My son started taking the buttons off my shirt. He began to work his way down to the bottom button, starting at the top button.

At the same time, he was removing the buttons from my dress, I noticed how cool the car's air conditioner felt against my skin. My nipples were rendered even more sensitive by it. The last button was unbuttoned when I felt it. Afterward, he took the time to undress me.

My son could do whatever he wanted to me in front of my nude body. He began stroking my body with his hands. He began stroking my tits. He continued to hold them in his hands like that. I threw my chest out in order for him to push even harder on my tits.

It was time for me to come out from under my skirt. My youngster was able to deduce the reasoning behind this.

In order to unzip his shorts, he dropped both of his hands. When he was unable to get to his zipper, I had to get up. I heard him unzipping his shorts. Still, I had his dick firmly lodged under my ass. My hips rose even higher.

Are you fine, honey? My spouse enquired, naturally.

"Are you having a hard time sitting on our son's lap?"

"Would you like me to slow down and park the car so you can relax?"

At the same time, Joel was taking his underwear off, and I could feel the tension building in his dick. Then I sat down on him again. He had his dick in my crotch and it was rubbing against my bare bottom.

I responded to my husband;

"Don't worry, honey, I guess I can make myself at home if I simply move around a little bit."

Then, I asked Joel;

"How are things going with you?

Is there anything else you require me to do so that you can feel relaxed?

Joel placed his hands on my hips, one on each side.

"Mom, if you'd just raise your head a bit so I can get a better position."

The words my son used made sense to me.

As high as I could, I raised my genitals into the air and held them there for a while. My hip felt a numbing sensation as one of his hands slipped off of it. It was clear to me what he was doing. I began to re-enter Joel's embrace. I was greeted by the head of his dick as soon as I was lowering my hip. I lowered my shoulders even further so that my husband won't know that I am undressed. He could only see my head slightly.

My pussy was simply slid into Joel's dick as I lower my hip further. The head of my son's dick was opening wide the opening of my pussy as I was lowering myself into it. I let out a low moan. That's what I ended up doing.

My husband gave me a sympathetic glance behind the wheel when he heard my sound, which was unknown to him that I was gently moaning.

"You don't want me to stop? Are you sure?" Asked, my husband.

As I lowered myself until I felt my son's dick bottom out in my pussy.

"No, no, don't stop, I want you to keep going. I'm good for the next half hour or so. What about you Joel, are you good for the next half hour? I said"

"Yeah mom, I made sure I was in a comfortable position before you sat back down on me."

For a brief moment, I must stand. *"Is that all right, Mom?"*

When it comes to rising up, do you want me to join you? I asked my son.

No. If you just stay on my lap, I positioned myself so I would have no problem. My son responded by raising his hips and ramming his dick deeper into me while saying that. I was almost there at the time.

"It's time for me to settle in." When I moved my ass around, I made his penis go around inside of me even more. I caught a glimpse of my husband's face as I rode my son's dick.

Joel continued to exert maximum pressure on my pussy. Only if my husband knew. Here I am, bare-chested, fucking my son behind my spouse.

"How soon after Joel moves into his dorm do you think we can see him?" I asked my husband, just to engage him, and for him not to be suspicious.

My husband replied, *"You can go see him without me if you don't mind the drive because of my job schedule."*

I got even hungrier as I was talking to my husband while my son's dick was deep inside me. It's fine if you don't show up every time, and don't worry about it. The more I can make it to our son, the better. That sounds OK right?

Joel responded; *"Mom, you're welcome to visit as often as you like."* I think it'll be even better if more of you come.

When he was done talking, he shoved me hard. He whispered to my ears, "How soon do you suppose you'll cum?"

"Really soon, Joel," I said

I began swiping my ass against his crotch. My only moving part was my groin. In order to keep my spouse from figuring out what we were doing, I kept my head immobile.

An orgasm was imminent. When Joel's hands were no longer on my hips, I put them on my tits. It was too much for me to take when my son put his hands on my tits. I was slammed by wave after wave as they rolled over me. I was unable to do anything but stiffen my muscles.

Approximately thirty seconds elapsed between. One of my best and most satisfying orgasms. I sank into my son's arms, exhausted.

My experience with Joel wasn't over yet. He kept shoving his genitalia into my crotch (He kept thrusting his dick in me). His legs sprang out in front of him. My son began firing his cum deep inside me. It was energizing for me. It was quite cozy. Until he emptied me of his cum, I remained still. Both of us were exhausted by the experience.

A notice (Billboard) says an eatery can be found about 10 miles down the road.

Do you guys mind? My husband asked.

Joel answered, "*Yeah, Dad, I could eat something.*" I turned around to see Joel staring back at me. The man was beaming at me. I'm curious about your thoughts, Mom. Is there anything you'd want to eat?

A hot dog or anything might do the trick for me, but I'm quite full.

I went down to pick up my pants that had fallen on the car's floor mat. My son's dick fell out of me as I bent over to pick them up. I pulled up the panties with my feet, which I inserted into the pants' legs. Before, I dragged them over my pussy and slapped them on. My son got horny again, he went and stuck his finger in me again. I gave him a playful slap on his hand. He took his finger out of me and I pulled my panties up. I started buttoning up my dress. He put his dick back in his pants and zipped up.

I asked my husband a question; *"After dinner, how far are we from our destination?"*

My husband chimed in. "It would take around two and a half hours."

Do you guys think you can manage that?"

"I'm not going to complain, I can cope," I assured my husband.

"I'll sit on Joel's lap for another two hours if he'll have me."

Then, Joel, how are things going with you, and would you be able to cope with me sitting on your lap for the next 2 hours? I asked"

"I thought the first two hours passed by rather quickly, too. As fast as or perhaps faster, I expect the following two hours to go likewise. Joel responded"

"I was expecting at least one of you to voice your displeasure by now," My husband said.

"Are there any issues that you'd like to raise son?" I asked Joel after telling my husband I had no displeasure"

"Mom, even if the ride went on forever, I wouldn't complain," Joel said.

The next two hours are going to be fantastic for you I promise he said.

Thank you, son, I can't wait to experience another 2 hours ride on your lap at the back seat.

…Continue to Series 2

Check out the continuation of this story in the second book in the series The Road Trip 2 (Mother and Son's Secret 2).

Thank You!

Free Bonus

Grab My "At The Beach (Erotic Romance Story)" Ebook For FREE!

Today you can grab your copy of my Free Erotic Romance story e-book titled – **At The Beach**. Best of all, it won't cost you a thing.

Download and Subscribe for Free book, giveaways, and new releases by **Karena Donger.**

Click the image above to **Download the Book**, and also Subscribe for Free books, giveaways, and new releases by me.
Or Follow the link below;

https://mayobook.com/karenadonger

As my subscriber, you will enjoy more free books exclusive to subscribers only, plus **Free Giveaways**. Wait no further, join my growing number of book lovers, and let's connect.

About The Author

I'm a romance writer and I've been writing for 10+ years. I write dark and romantic erotica. I have a penchant for romance. I also have a fondness for writing stories that inspire, and a love for the genre of romantic fiction. I write dark and erotic romance because I love the power of darkness and the eroticism that comes with it. I love the passion and the desire. I love the way a man will stop at nothing to get what he wants.

I also write fantasy and contemporary romance because I love the magic and adventure of it, coupled with the modern world and the characters in it. I love the modern family and modern relationships.

I have always loved reading romance novels, and now I am writing them too. I hope to share my love of romance with readers through my writing.

Visit https://mayobook.com/karenadonger to download my Free Erotic story **"At The Beach"** Today!

Other Books

1. The Road Trip (Mother and Son's Secret Book 1)

2. The Road Trip 2 (Mother and Son's Secret Book 2)

3. Our Secret (Mother and Son's Secret Book 3)

4. Our Secret 2 (Mother and Son's Secret Book 4)

5. The Road Trip Secret, Complete Series Box Set (Mother and Son's Secret)